To Our Sweet Baby Oscar,
Love,
Grandma

We love you so
much.
Grandma

for
Marcia Paschkis
and
Cecilia Jensen

Henry Holt and Company, LLC
Publishers since 1866
115 West 18th Street
New York, New York 10011
www.henryholt.com

Distributed in Canada by H. B. Fenn and Company Ltd.

Library of Congress Cataloging-in-Publication Data
Lord, Janet.
Here comes Grandma! / Janet Lord; illustrated by Julie Paschkis.—1st ed.
p.   cm.
Summary: Grandma is coming to visit and she will use any possible method of transport,
including a horse and a hot air balloon, to get there.
ISBN-13: 978-0-8050-7666-0   ISBN-10: 0-8050-7666-2
[1. Transportation—Fiction. 2. Grandmothers—Fiction.] I. Paschkis, Julie, ill. II. Title.
PZ7.L8775He 2005   [E]—dc22   2004022179

First Edition—2005 / Designed by Amy Manzo Toth
Printed in the United States of America on acid-free paper. ∞

1 3 5 7 9 10 8 6 4 2

The artist used Winsor & Newton gouaches on Arches paper to create the illustrations for this book.

Here Comes Grandma!

Janet Lord

ILLUSTRATED BY **Julie Paschkis**

Henry Holt and Company • New York

Here comes Grandma!

I'm coming to see you.

I'll pull on my boots
and walk a long way to see you.

I'll pedal my bicycle
and zip over the hills to see you.

Here comes Grandma!

I'll leap on a horse
and clip-clop through town to see you.

I'll drive a car
and vroom down the road to see you.

I'll hop a train
and ride the rails to see you.

Here comes Grandma!

I'll slip on my skis
and whoosh down the mountain to see you.

I'll sail a balloon
and breeze over the treetops to see you.

Here comes Grandma!

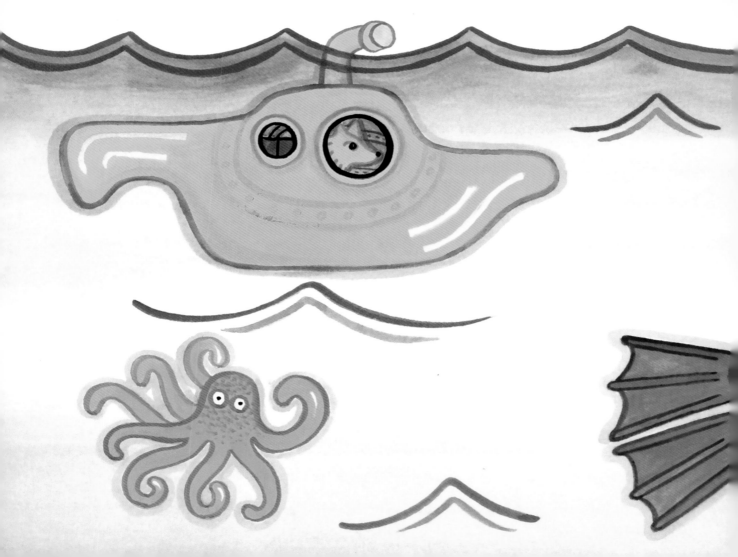

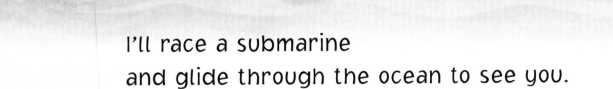

I'll race a submarine
and glide through the ocean to see you.

I'll fly a plane
and zoom through the clouds to see you.

Here comes Grandma. I'm coming to see you!

And when I get there . . .

. . . we'll whirl and twirl,
and laugh and sing,
and I'll give you a
great
big
hug!